Creativity in Environmental Protection

商務印書館(香港)有限公司
http://www.commercialpress.com.hk

CENGAGE
Learning™

Australia • Brazil • Japan • Korea • Mexico • Singapore • Spain • United Kingdom • United States

Director of Content Development:
Anita Raducanu
Series Editor: Rob Waring
Editorial Manager: Bryan Fletcher

Associate Development Editors:
Victoria Forrester, Catherine McCue
責任編輯：黃家麗

出版：

商務印書館（香港）有限公司
香港筲箕灣耀興道3號東匯廣場8樓

Cengage Learning
Units 808-810, 8th floor,
Tins Enterprises Centre,
777 Lai Chi Kok Road, Cheung Sha Wan,
Kowloon, Hong Kong

網址：http://www.commercialpress.com.hk

http://www.cengageasia.com

發行：香港聯合書刊物流有限公司
　　　香港新界大埔汀麗路36號中華商務
　　　印刷大廈3字樓

印刷：中華商務彩色印刷有限公司
版次：2010年3月第1版第2次印刷

ISBN: 978-962-07-1877-9

出版説明

本館一向倡導優質閱讀，近年連續推出以"Q"為標誌的優質英語學習系列(*Quality English Learning*)，其中《Black Cat 優質英語階梯閱讀》，讀者反應令人鼓舞，先後共推出超過60本。

為進一步推動閱讀，本館引入Cengage 出版之*Footprint Library*，使用*National Geographic*的圖像及語料，編成百科英語階梯閱讀系列，有別於Black Cat 古典文學閱讀，透過現代真實題材，百科英語語境能幫助讀者認識今日的世界各事各物，擴闊視野，提高認識及表達英語的能力。

本系列屬non-fiction (非虛構故事類)讀本，結合閱讀、視像和聽力三種學習功能，是一套三合一多媒介讀本，每本書的英文文章以headwords寫成，headwords 選收自以下數據庫的語料：*Collins Cobuild The Bank of English*、*British National Corpus* 及 *BYU Corpus of American English* 等，並配上精彩照片，另加一張video/audio 兩用DVD。編排由淺入深，按級提升，只要讀者堅持學習，必能有效提高英語溝通能力。

商務印書館(香港)有限公司
編輯部

使用説明

百科英語階梯閱讀分四級，共八本書，是彩色有影有聲書，每本有英語文章供閱讀，根據數據庫如 *Collins Cobuild The Bank of English*、*British National Corpus* 及 *BYU Corpus of American English* 選收常用字詞編寫，配彩色照片及一張video/audio 兩用DVD，結合閱讀、聆聽、視像三種學習方式。

讀者可使用本書：

 學習新詞彙，並透過延伸閱讀(Expansion Reading)
練習速讀技巧

 聆聽錄音提高聽力，模仿標準英語讀音

 看短片做練習，以提升綜合理解能力

Grammar Focus解釋語法重點，後附練習題，供讀者即時複習所學，書內其他練習題，有助讀者掌握學習技巧如 scanning, prediction, summarising, identifying the main idea

中英對照生詞表設於書後，既不影響讀者閱讀正文，又具備參考作用

Contents 目錄

The CD-ROM contains a video and full recording of the text

CD-ROM 包括短片和錄音

Words to Know

This story starts in the U.S. cities of Sacramento and Borrego Springs, California. It then moves on to villages in Africa and around the world.

 Solar Cooking. Read the sentences. Then complete the paragraph with the correct form of the <u>underlined</u> words.

> <u>Cardboard</u> is very thick paper that is usually used for making boxes.
> A <u>cooker</u> is a piece of equipment that is used to cook food.
> <u>Solar</u> refers to something that is of or related to the sun.
> A <u>workshop</u> is a meeting of people to learn more about a particular subject.

This story is about a way of using (1)_____ power to cook food. A group called 'Solar Cookers International' has developed a (2)_____ that is made of a thick paper. This paper, or (3)_____, is covered with a reflective material which uses the sun's light to cook food. (4)_____ are now being held around the world to teach people how to use the sun to cook food.

Villagers at a Solar Cooking Workshop

solar cooker

2

B Solar Cookers Help People. Read the paragraph. Then complete the definitions with the correct form of the words or phrases.

Developing countries have a number of significant problems. In some places, large areas are being deforested by people who need wood for energy. Charcoal and other fuels that people burn for cooking can cause health problems. The lack of safe drinking water and large number of waterborne diseases are also big issues. Unless water is pasteurised, it may carry diseases and make people ill. Microbiologist Bob Metcalf and writer Eleanor Shimeall are teaching people how to fix these problems by using solar cookers in their everyday lives.

1. A scientist who studies very small living things, such as bacteria, is a m_____.

2. The cutting down of trees in large areas is called d_____.

3. C_____ is a hard, black substance that is burned for energy.

4. W_____ means to be carried or transferred by water.

5. A d_____ c_____ is a nation that is economically weak but growing.

6. F_____ are substances that release energy when burned.

7. To heat something at a controlled temperature in order to kill disease-causing elements is to p_____.

cardboard

reflective material

It's a cool but sunny day in Borrego Springs, California. As Eleanor Shimeall prepares to cook her meal, she opens the door and steps outside of her home. You see, this woman doesn't cook inside her kitchen – she cooks outdoors! She walks over to a strange-looking piece of **equipment**[1] and opens a glass door to put in her bread. She then opens the lower part of another glass and wood construction and says, 'I'm going to check on this chicken and rice and see how it's cooking.' As she takes off the top of the pot, she can see that the dish is cooking nicely. 'Ah, it's doing a good job,' she says.

Shimeall's meal looks delicious; however, there's one **remarkable**[2] thing about her cooking method. Unlike most people, she isn't using electricity, gas, charcoal, or wood to cook her food. Instead, Shimeall is using the sun to make her meal, and she's done it almost every day for more than 20 years. She cooks with solar power!

---

[1] **equipment:** things used for a particular purpose
[2] **remarkable:** unusual or special and therefore surprising

A Solar Cooker

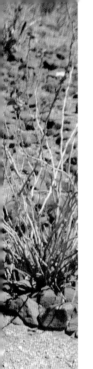

A solar cooker is a type of **stove**[1] that needs only the light from the sun, or sunshine, to cook food. It can cook a delicious meal even if the air temperature is not very hot. Solar cookers can be used to cook meat, fish, grains, and vegetables. They can cook just about anything that can be cooked on a normal stove.

This method of cooking is becoming popular among people who are concerned about the environment. However, they aren't the only people interested in this unusual invention. In developing countries around the world, solar cookers have the potential to save lives. According to one expert, people around the world may soon not have enough traditional fuels. He explains in his own words, 'With sunshine you have an **alternative**[2] to fire. And that's important for two and a half billion people to learn about because they're running out of traditional fuels.'

---

[1]**stove:** a piece of kitchen equipment, usually containing an oven, used to cook food
[2]**alternative:** another choice

A Traditional Stove

Dr Bob Metcalf is a microbiologist and a **founding member**[1] of Solar Cookers International, or SCI for short. He, along with Eleanor Shimeall and her husband, helped to create the small nonprofit organisation which is based in Sacramento, California. For the last 15 years, SCI has promoted solar cooking around the world, especially in the developing countries of Africa.

The organisation's goals focus primarily on two areas. They want to help stop the terrible **deforestation**[2] which is occurring in some countries, and they want to make women's lives easier. The problem of deforestation is often due to the demand for trees to use as fuel. But how does an organisation like SCI help women? How can women's lives be improved with solar cooking?

---

[1]**founding member:** one of the people who started an organisation; the first in a group
[2]**deforestation:** the cutting down of trees in a large area

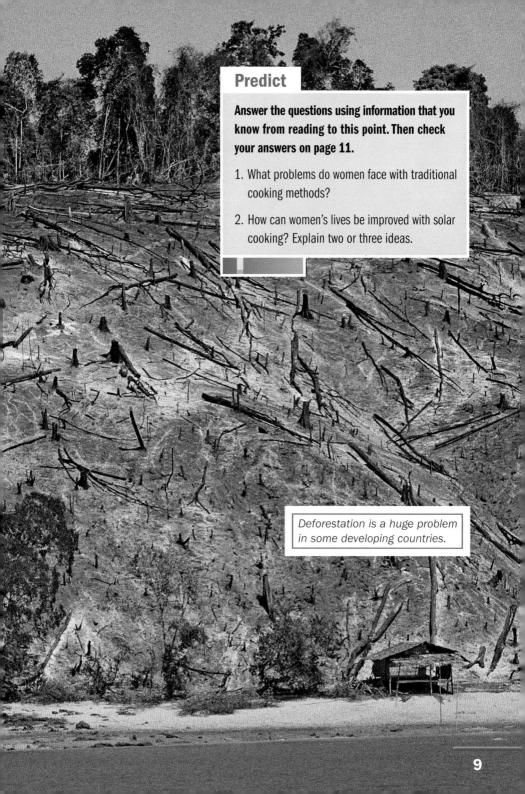

Predict

Answer the questions using information that you know from reading to this point. Then check your answers on page 11.

1. What problems do women face with traditional cooking methods?

2. How can women's lives be improved with solar cooking? Explain two or three ideas.

Deforestation is a huge problem in some developing countries.

In order to help people better understand the **issue**,[1] Dr Metcalf describes the lifestyle of many women in parts of Africa. 'They have to walk about two to three miles or so to collect wood,' he says. 'And then they have to tend the fire. And the smoke from that fire, it burns their eyes and **chokes their lungs**.'[2]

According to the **World Health Organization**,[3] this indoor pollution has been linked to the deaths of two million women and children each year. With help from other human aid groups, Solar Cookers International has already trained more than 22,000 families. They have taught these families how to cook their traditional foods with the sun.

---

[1]**issue:** an important subject that people discuss
[2]**choke (one's) lungs:** cause breathing problems by blocking airways in the breathing organs in the chest called the 'lungs'
[3]**World Health Organization (WHO):** an agency of the United Nations that works to improve global health conditions

But does solar cooking really work? Does it really cook food well? Solar Cookers International thinks so! The group organises workshops on cooking with solar cookers. In these workshops, the women learn how to set up and use the solar cooking equipment. They also get a chance to actually prepare foods on the cookers. The women make a wide range of dishes including soups, rice, potatoes, and bread.

After a day of preparing the foods, the users are finally able to taste their 'solar-powered food'. 'Oh, this is good,' says one woman as she tries the food from a workshop. 'It's very good,' she continues, 'The **consistency**[1] is good; the **texture**[2] is fine.' She then concludes with a smile, 'No problem!'

The fact that the solar cooker looks just like a cardboard box surprises many of the women. One of the cooks says, 'We're all amazed that a cardboard box can cook.' After each workshop, attendees are given their own **portable**[3] solar 'cook **kits**'[4] to take home. They are then expected to use the kits to help them with their daily tasks. The simple cookers cost about five dollars, last almost two years, and work exactly like the more costly kits.

---

[1]**consistency:** the degree of thickness, softness, etc.
[2]**texture:** the way sth feels according to sense of taste or touch
[3]**portable:** movable; capable of being carried or moved around
[4]**kit:** a set of things, such as tools, used for a particular purpose

How does the solar cooker work? Dr Metcalf explains: 'Shiny things direct the sunshine onto a dark pot that then **absorbs**[1] the sunshine, and changes that light energy into heat energy.' He then talks about how this heat energy becomes caught in the plastic bag or window that covers the pot in a solar cooker: 'And heat energy doesn't get out of the clear plastic bag; it doesn't get out of the window.'

Solar cooking is a simple yet **brilliant**[2] idea that has several advantages. Not only is it a safe way to cook foods without traditional fuels, but SCI says that it's also an effective way of making water pure and safe to drink. These two capabilities make the solar cooker a major benefit for developing countries.

---

[1] **absorb:** slowly take in
[2] **brilliant:** extremely clever or skilful

Dr Metcalf explains the importance of solar cookers in making water safe to **consume**.[1] 'Six thousand people a day are going to die of waterborne diseases in developing countries. If you heat water to 65° Celsius, 149° Fahrenheit, you can pasteurise water and make it safe to drink.'

Solar Cookers International has developed a useful little measuring tool in order to help people to know when water is safe to drink. The measuring tool, which uses **wax**,[2] is designed to be placed in water that's on the cooker. Dr Metcalf explains how the measuring tool works. 'If the water gets hot enough to melt this wax,' he says, 'the water has reached **pasteurisation**[3] temperatures.' Basically, users can look at the simple clear container. If the wax is solid, the water is not safe. If the wax has melted, the people can drink the water and not get sick.

---

[1] **consume:** to eat or drink
[2] **wax:** a soft substance used in candles
[3] **pasteurisation:** a heating process that kills disease-causing elements

Solar Cookers International has been very successful at making the lives of African women easier with their solar cooker workshops. Similar solar projects are now getting started in a number of countries. From Nepal to Nicaragua, solar cooking projects are helping people in nearly every country in the developing world. Some communities are even **experimenting**[1] with solar cookers for large volumes of food. But SCI is not satisfied with just helping these people. Their goal is to increase the use of solar cookers everywhere.

Dr Metcalf is aware of the importance of providing solar cooking **technology**[2] to the places that need it the most. He explains in his own words. 'Science is supposed to help and benefit all of mankind,' he says, 'and [we've] got something that is good science that could help two and a half billion people in the world.' To this he then adds, 'There's a great need [to share the] information that these things work.' Dr Metcalf wants to spread the news about the ease and safety of solar cooking. Hopefully someday soon, everyone will feel the way that one workshop attendee did. At the end of the training, she just smiled and said, 'OK, solar cooker!'

---

[1] **experiment:** to try out a new idea or method to see what happens
[2] **technology:** the knowledge, equipment, and methods used in science and industry

Summarise

Imagine you are teaching one of the workshops. Write or talk about the importance and the benefits of the solar cooker.

After You Read

1. What does the word 'remarkable' mean on page 4?
   A. strange
   B. special
   C. serious
   D. standard

2. Which of the following does Eleanor Shimealls use to cook her food?
   A. wind
   B. gas
   C. sun
   D. wood

3. Why does solar cooking have the potential to save lives?
   A. It can replace disappearing fuels.
   B. It's safer than cooking with wood.
   C. It's easier than traditional cooking.
   D. It cooks meals faster than other stoves.

4. Which of the following is one of the main goals of Solar Cookers International?
   A. To make everyone in the world use solar cooking.
   B. To teach people the benefits of alternative fuels.
   C. To give better lives to women in developing nations.
   D. To stop the use of electric stoves.

5. Wood is an inconvenient and sometimes dangerous fuel.
   A. True
   B. False

6. How many years does one solar cooker last?
   A. five
   B. one
   C. twenty-two
   D. two

7. Some African women expressed the view that the solar cooker:
   A. doesn't look like a stove.
   B. doesn't make tasty food.
   C. isn't compact enough.
   D. can't be used on a rainy day.

8. What helps energy to get trapped in the solar cooker?
   A. a dark pot
   B. a cardboard box
   C. a shiny thing
   D. a plastic bag

9. What does 'it' refer to on page 16?
   A. waterborne disease
   B. Fahrenheit
   C. water
   D. a solar cooker

10. A measuring tool that uses wax _____ make water safe.
   A. doesn't
   B. helps
   C. should
   D. tries to

11. What does Dr Metcalf believe about the role of science in society?
   A. Science should be used to help people.
   B. Science doesn't support mankind enough.
   C. Society needs more organisations like his.
   D. Society should support science more.

12. What is the main purpose of the final paragraph?
   A. To introduce Dr Metcalf's goals.
   B. To show that people appreciate solar cookers.
   C. To give an example from Nepal.
   D. To explain the cookers are not successful yet.

The History of Solar Cooking

For most of human history, people did not cook their food. They simply ate it the way it was found. Thousands of years ago, people learned how to use fire for cooking purposes. However, humans have long been interested in using the heat from the sun to cook their food as well. An ancient group of people called the Essenes lived in the northern part of Africa about 2,000 years ago. Records indicate that they heated thin pieces of bread on rocks that were warmed by the sun.

The first modern experiments in solar cooking began during the 1700s. At this time, glass was becoming more widely available and people began to use it for windows. It soon became clear that when the sun passed through a glass window into a closed room, the air in the room became warmer.

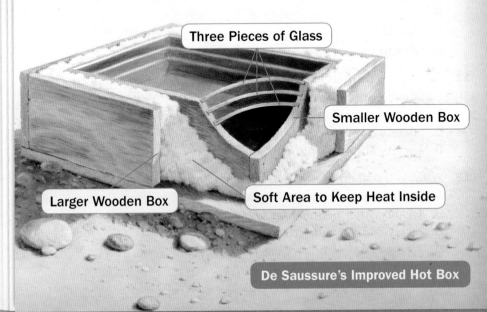

Three Pieces of Glass

Smaller Wooden Box

Larger Wooden Box

Soft Area to Keep Heat Inside

De Saussure's Improved Hot Box

4.5 billion years ago	1767	1891

100 B.C.	1830s	1970s

Solar energy first reaches the earth.	De Saussure's glass boxes heat air to 87.5°C.	American Clarence Kemp invents the first solar water heater.

The Essenes 'cook' bread on hot rocks.	Sir John Herschel uses solar cookers while exploring South Africa.	The governments of China and India begin to promote solar cooking.

A Time Line of Solar Energy

In the 1760s, a French-Swiss scientist, Horace de Saussure, became interested in why this happened and how much heat could be produced this way. In 1767, he conducted an experiment which measured the temperature changes in boxes as they were heated by the sun.

De Saussure's first experiment involved a set of five small glass boxes, each one placed inside of the other. The largest box was 12 inches by 12 inches and the smallest box was 2 inches by 2 inches. He placed the boxes on a black wooden table. He used a black surface because he knew it would hold the heat of the sun rather than reflecting it away. After several hours, he checked the temperatures in the boxes. The outer box was coolest and the smallest box in the centre was warmest. The temperature in the inner box was 87.5°C. De Saussure had placed some fruits in this container and found that the fruits were actually cooked by the heat in the box. Later, he built a more efficient heat box using wood and glass and was able to raise the temperature to 109°C. This is well above the boiling point of water, which is 100°C. This improved cooker later became known as a 'hot box' and was the basis for many further solar experiments.

Word Count: 361
Time: _____

Words to Know

This story is set in the United States in the state of Iowa. It happens in a town called Spirit Lake, which is north of the city of Des Moines.

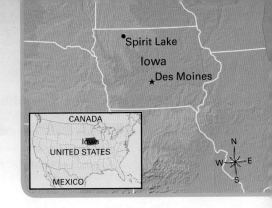

A **Energy Past and Present.** Read the paragraph. Then match each word or phrase with the correct definition.

Fossil fuels can be used to make energy, but they're bad for the environment and their amounts are limited. In windy places, some people now use wind turbines to make cleaner energy. This energy can be used immediately or sent to an electricity grid and sold. Wind turbines are very tall and have huge wind blades that come together at a hub. These high structures must be set in strong foundations so that they don't fall over.

1. fossil fuel _____	**a.** a system that supplies electrical power to a large area
2. wind turbine _____	**b.** the centre of something shaped like a wheel
3. electricity grid _____	**c.** a machine that produces power by using wind
4. blade _____	**d.** a thin, wide part of a machine used to push air or water
5. hub _____	**e.** the hard, solid base that supports a structure
6. foundation _____	**f.** a material that releases heat when it's burned to provide energy

The Fossil Fuels Coal and Oil

pieces of coal

barrels of oil

B **Life in Iowa.** Read the facts about Iowa. Then write the correct form of each <u>underlined</u> word next to the correct definition.

The <u>countryside</u> of Iowa doesn't have many hills so it's very flat.
Farmers in Iowa grow many different <u>crops</u> to eat and sell.
Iowa farmers store winter food for animals in <u>silos</u>.
Some parts of Iowa have strong storms called <u>tornados</u>.

1. a large, round building on a farm used to store food and products: _____

2. land that is not in towns or cities and has farms, fields, forests, etc.: _____

3. foods that are grown in large amounts: _____

4. an extremely strong and dangerous wind that blows in a circle and often destroys things as it moves along: _____

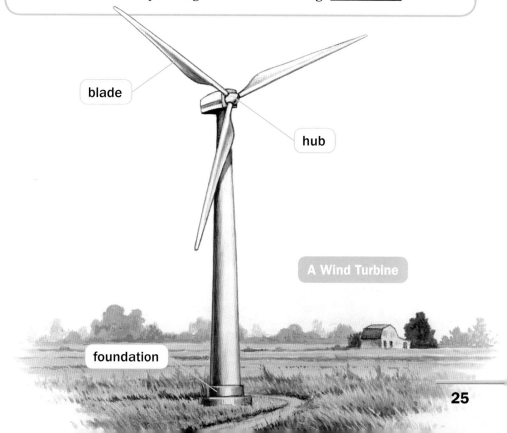

blade

hub

A Wind Turbine

foundation

A round the town of Spirit Lake in the U.S. state of Iowa, the weather is very windy. The land is very flat, and the wind blows across it a lot of the time. For the people who live in the area, it's not always easy to live with the windy weather.

One **school district**,[1] however, is using the wind in order to get an advantage. The school officials in the town of Spirit Lake have built two wind turbines right next to their schools. These turbines are helping the schools to save energy – and money.

---

[1]**school district:** an official area which has a certain number of schools

Jim Tirevold, who works with the turbines, explains how much money the turbines have saved the school district. He says: 'The little turbine, since it's been **paid off**,[1] has saved the district $81,530.' That's a lot of money!

Spirit Lake's wind power programme began in 1993, when the school district built its first wind turbine. This was the first turbine used to power a school in this part of the United States. Since that time, the school has **constructed**[2] a second wind turbine. Together, the two turbines could save the district as much as $140,000 a year in energy costs.

[1]**pay off:** to pay for sth completely
[2]**construct:** to build or make

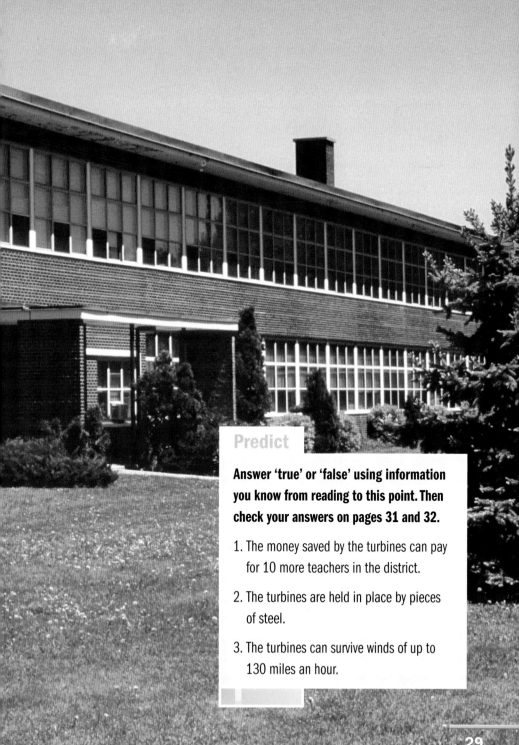

Predict

Answer 'true' or 'false' using information you know from reading to this point. Then check your answers on pages 31 and 32.

1. The money saved by the turbines can pay for 10 more teachers in the district.

2. The turbines are held in place by pieces of steel.

3. The turbines can survive winds of up to 130 miles an hour.

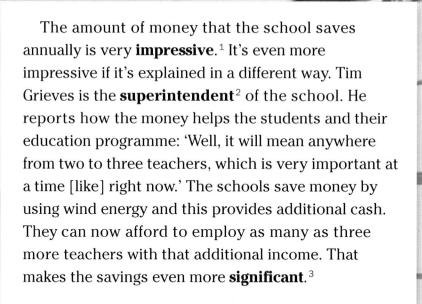

The amount of money that the school saves annually is very **impressive**.[1] It's even more impressive if it's explained in a different way. Tim Grieves is the **superintendent**[2] of the school. He reports how the money helps the students and their education programme: 'Well, it will mean anywhere from two to three teachers, which is very important at a time [like] right now.' The schools save money by using wind energy and this provides additional cash. They can now afford to employ as many as three more teachers with that additional income. That makes the savings even more **significant**.[3]

[1]**impressive:** great in size or degree
[2]**superintendent:** a person who manages a school in the U.S.
[3]**significant:** large enough to be important

But what about the energy-making machines themselves? How are they designed? To understand this, it's best to actually go inside a turbine. From the inside, it's clear just how big the turbines really are. Tirevold takes a visitor into the larger, newer turbine. As the two men look up at the huge structure, Tirevold talks about its size. 'This turbine stands 180 feet to the hub height,' he explains.

The turbine itself is held in place by many steel rods. These rods go 25 feet down into a solid foundation. This is done because the wind turbines must be very strong and able to **withstand**,[1] or survive, very strong winds. But just how strong? 'What type of a wind could this withstand?' asks the visitor as he looks around the turbine. 'It's rated to **stand up to**[2] 130-mile-an-hour winds,' Tirevold replies. The strength of the turbines is especially important in this part of Iowa, where **tornados**[3] can – and do – occur. In extremely strong winds, the huge blades of the wind turbines are designed to shut down, or stop working.

[1]**withstand:** to survive sth without being changed or damaged
[2]**stand up to:** not to be damaged or harmed by sth
[3]**tornado:** extremely strong wind that blows in a circle

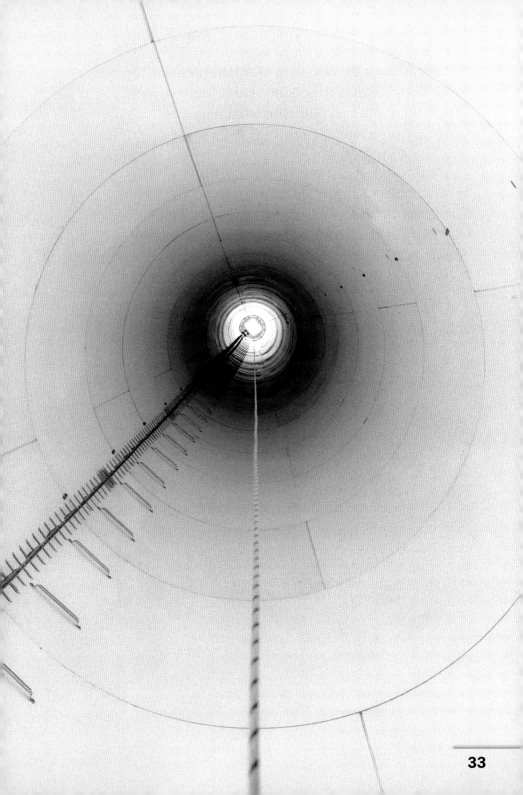

The turbines are also very **efficient**[1] at using the wind. They are able to produce energy in winds of just eight miles an hour. But what happens to all of this energy? Where does it go?

The smaller of the two turbines at the Spirit Lake School sends its power directly to the school itself. The larger turbine sends its power to the local electricity grid where it can be used by the energy company. By doing this, the little school district is able to sell the extra energy that the turbines produce.

---

[1]**efficient:** working well without wasting time and energy

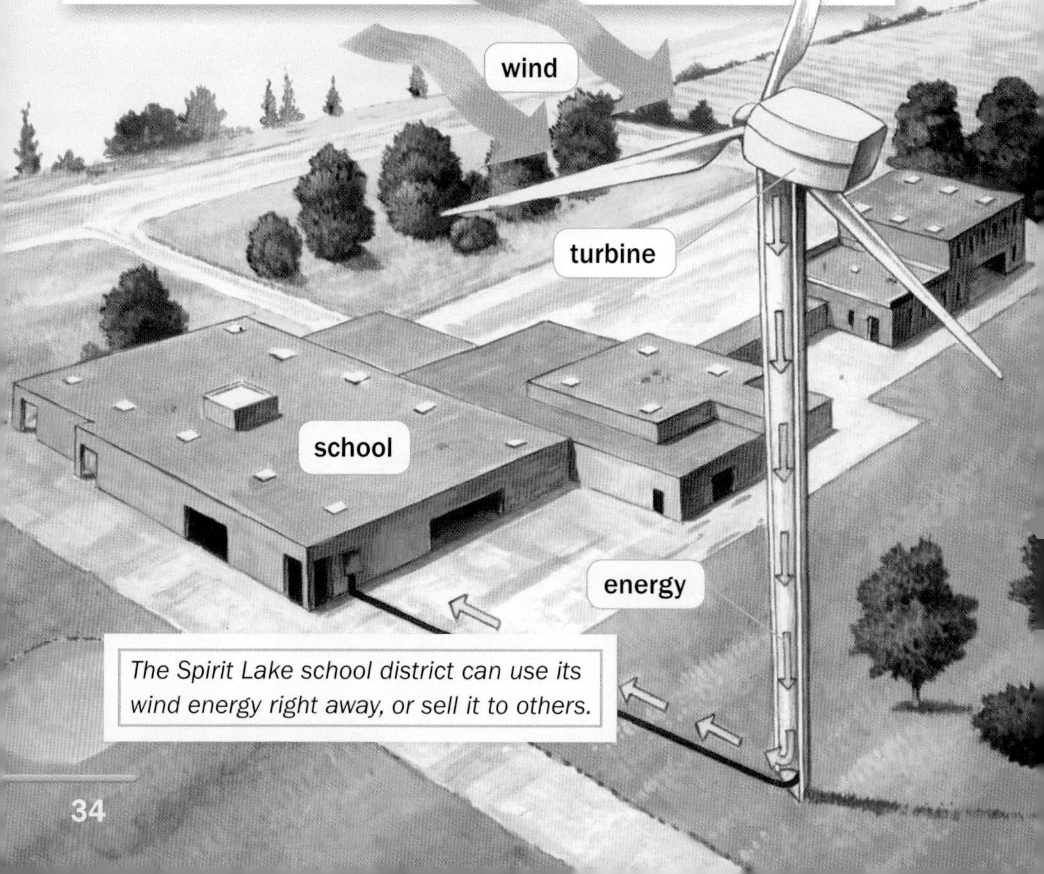

wind

turbine

school

energy

The Spirit Lake school district can use its wind energy right away, or sell it to others.

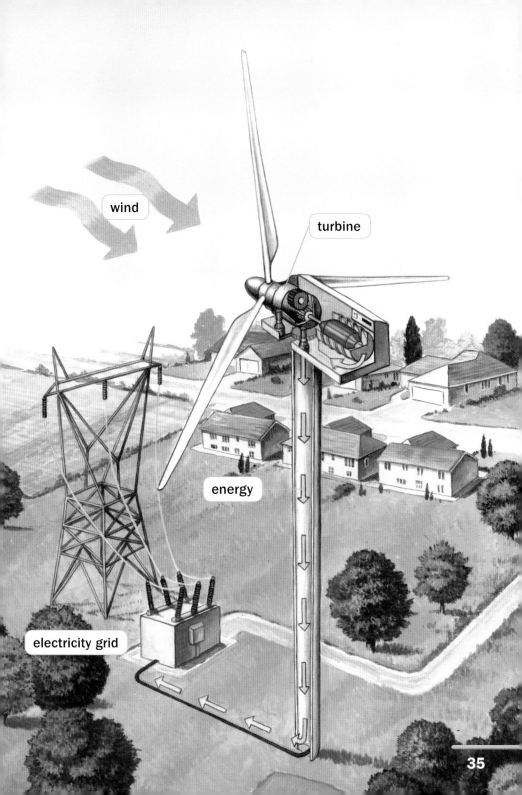

wind

turbine

energy

electricity grid

The schools aren't the only ones who are making money in the energy business. The community around them is also getting involved with wind power production. In the countryside south of the Spirit Lake schools, there are more turbines. They stand near the big silos on local farms. In this area, 65 farmers have recently allowed energy companies to build wind turbines directly next to their fields. Now, the farmers can make money from the wind, just as they do from selling their crops.

Farmer Charles Goodman thinks he'll make an extra $6,000 a year from the three turbines on his farm. For him, windy weather means extra money. How does Goodman feel about it? On a visit to the farm, one person decided to find out. 'So when you see the wind **kicking pretty good**[1] like it is, that's money in your pocket, right?' asks the visitor. 'I smile all the time when the wind's blowing like this,' Goodman replies with a little laugh. Wind power seems to be a **valuable**[2] 'crop' for Spirit Lake's farmers as well.

---

[1]**kicking pretty good:** *(slang)* moving fast
[2]**valuable:** worth a lot of money

This piece of the Iowa countryside is just 27 miles long, but it now has 257 wind turbines. These turbines provide enough energy to power a city like Des Moines – that's 71,000 homes!

The turbines are also providing more than just power. In the Spirit Lake schools, wind power is used for teaching as well. Jan Bolluyt is a **physics**[1] teacher in the school district. He can't imagine why schools wouldn't want to use wind power. He explains: 'When I talk [to students] about force, energy, and electricity, they see that we're producing it right here.' The wind power programme actually provides students with a real-life **model**[2] of the subjects they are studying at school.

[1]**physics:** the scientific study of natural forces, such as energy, heat, and light
[2]**model:** a smaller copy of an object showing how the object works; example

The effects of using a cleaner fuel supply at the school have been impressive. The teachers encourage students to keep detailed records about the wind power programme. They write down the amounts of fossil fuels, such as coal, that the school no longer needs for energy. This information clearly **indicates**[1] that wind power is an alternative form of energy that can be good for the environment. It significantly reduces the production of dirty, dangerous gases that damage the air and the trees. Bolluyt reports how much the programme is helping the environment: 'We're talking [about reducing] tons of **carbon dioxide**.[2] We're talking [about reducing] tons of **sulphur dioxide**.[3] We're talking [about saving] hundreds of trees. So, you know, it's not just a small thing.'

In this part of Iowa, people are using wind power to earn money and to learn about saving the environment. The people of Spirit Lake are using the power of the wind to ensure a better future for everyone!

---

[1]**indicate:** to show that sth is true or exists
[2]**carbon dioxide:** a gas that is produced when people and animals breathe out (CO_2)
[3]**sulphur dioxide:** a gas with a strong smell (SO_2)

Environmental Benefits of the Spirit Lake Wind Power Programme

Carbon Dioxide

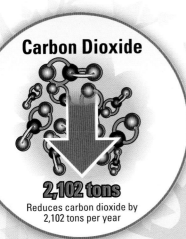

2,102 tons

Reduces carbon dioxide by
2,102 tons per year

Sulphur Dioxide

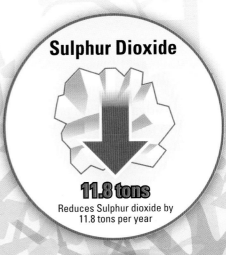

11.8 tons

Reduces Sulphur dioxide by
11.8 tons per year

Oil Use

4,000 barrels

Saves over 4,000 barrels
of oil per year

OR

Coal Use

1,107 tons

Saves 1,107 tons
of coal per year

Summarise

Imagine that you are a student at a Spirit Lake
school. Write or talk about the wind power
programme and the benefits of wind power.

After You Read

1. The wind blows across Spirit Lake _____ of the time.
   A. all
   B. most
   C. some
   D. none

2. 'An advantage' on page 26 can be replaced by:
   A. a power
   B. an assistance
   C. a benefit
   D. a help

3. What does Jim Trevold think about the wind turbine?
   A. It's small.
   B. It's expensive.
   C. It's weak.
   D. It's useful.

4. Why did the school build a second turbine?
   A. to get energy and save more money
   B. because the first wasn't powerful enough
   C. to show the students how to use wind
   D. because they had no electricity

5. What does 'it' refer to in Tim Grieves' comment on page 31?
   A. wind
   B. energy
   C. money
   D. education

6. The turbines create job opportunities.
   A. True
   B. False
   C. Not in text

7. In extremely high winds, the turbines:
   A. produce a lot of energy.
   B. turn off.
   C. have problems.
   D. go slowly.

8. What is the purpose of the steel rods?
   A. to support the turbines
   B. to withstand heavy rain
   C. to go 130 feet underground
   D. to help the wind get stronger

9. The electrical grid _____ power to be used later.
   A. creates
   B. keeps
   C. designs
   D. survives

10. What is the purpose of page 37?
   A. to show how the school has influenced the town
   B. to show the connection between turbines and silos
   C. to show how wind energy can affect the countryside
   D. to show that wind energy makes more money than farming

11. A suitable heading for page 38 is:
   A. Turbines Teach Students
   B. Physics Teacher Uses Turbines
   C. School Has Class Outside
   D. Students Love Wind Energy

12. What view is expressed by the teacher on page 40?
   A. Wind is a great fossil fuel.
   B. The school is protecting the environment.
   C. Recording data is necessary in science.
   D. The students should plant new trees.

HEINLE Times

(4) TIDAL POWER: YET ANOTHER ENERGY OPTION

People have been experimenting with alternative ways to make energy for a long time. More than a hundred years ago, people started placing turbines in rivers. The moving water turned the turbine and created power. More recently, companies have begun using the power of the wind to provide electrical energy. Wind farms are now a common sight in many areas of the world. Electricity grids that are connected to these turbines supply electricity to millions of people. Both of these methods avoid the use of fossil fuels and help create a cleaner environment.

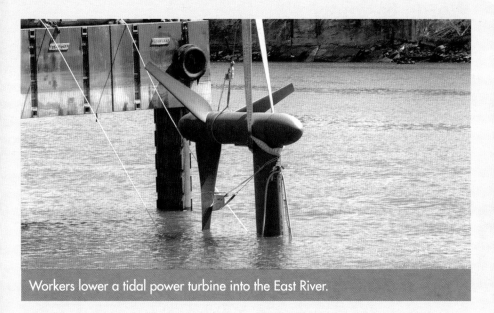

Workers lower a tidal power turbine into the East River.

In the past few years, however, there has been increased interest in another energy option on the coasts of the United States. People there now want to use the power of ocean tides, or the rise and fall of ocean water each day. Like wind power, tidal power provides a very clean energy supply. However, it does have one big advantage over wind power. Wind comes and goes and there is no way to control it. Tidal power is predictable and it occurs every day. People who are operating tidal power stations know exactly when the tide will come in and go out.

In some ways, tidal turbines are very similar to those used to make electricity from wind. For example, both types of turbine must have a very heavy foundation. Wind turbines need them because they are very tall and might fall over in high winds. Tidal turbines need them because they are placed in narrow openings on the ocean floor. In these places, the force of the moving water is extremely strong.

In other ways, the two types of turbines are quite different. The blades of a tidal turbine must be much stronger than those of a wind turbine. A company called Verdant Energy learned this lesson quickly. They built some model turbines for its project in New York City's East River. When they put the turbines into the river, the blades immediately broke off from the hub. The company had to design new, stronger blades before the project could continue.

 Word Count: 354
Time: _____

Words to Know

This story is set in South Africa. It happens in Karoo National Park. A national park is a special area where nature is protected.

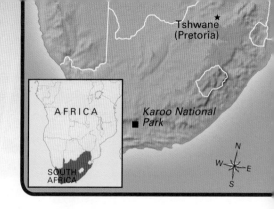

A **Wild Animals in Africa.** Read the sentences and label the pictures with the underlined words.

A <u>herd</u> is a large group of animals.

Africa has many wild animals like <u>elephants</u>, <u>zebras</u>, and <u>giraffes</u>.

People often find wild <u>animal tracks</u>, or footprints, in Africa.

1. _____

3. _____

2. _____

4. _____

5. _____

B **Conservation Technology.** Read the paragraph and notice the underlined words. Then answer the questions.

African Bushmen can track, or follow, animals very well. They can learn many things by tracking animals. However, the Bushmen can't always tell other people what they know. They don't always speak the same <u>language</u>. This story is about a <u>conservationist</u> called Louis Liebenberg. He is helping to protect Africa's wild animals. He has developed a new type of <u>technology</u> for getting information about the animals. It's a method that doesn't depend on spoken language. It's called the 'Cyber Tracker'.

1. What does **'language'** mean? _____

2. What does **'conservationist'** mean? _____

3. What does **'technology'** mean? _____

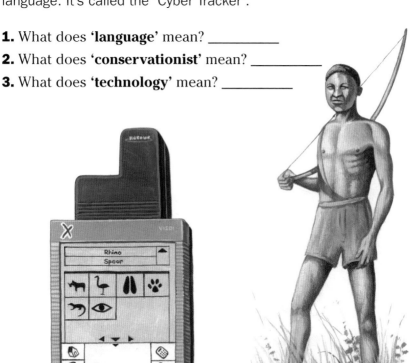

The Cyber Tracker — **An African Bushman**

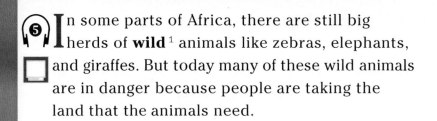

In some parts of Africa, there are still big herds of **wild**[1] animals like zebras, elephants, and giraffes. But today many of these wild animals are in danger because people are taking the land that the animals need.

It's a big problem that worries many **conservationists**.[2] Conservationists are people who protect wildlife and nature. Some conservationists are now leading a fight to save these animals.

---

[1]**wild:** living in a natural environment
[2]**conservationist:** a person who cares for and protects natural resources and the environment

Louis Liebenberg is one of the conservationists who is trying to save the wildlife in Africa. He feels that having good information about the animals is very important for success. 'The most important thing is to try and get an understanding of what's happening out there,' he says.

Liebenberg reports that people need to know more about animals. He says that people need to understand what happens to plants and animals over time. Are they increasing or decreasing in numbers? What plants are the animals eating?

Summarise

What does Liebenberg mean?

1. Summarise the first paragraph in one sentence.

2. Summarise the second paragraph in one sentence.

African Bushmen may be able to help conservationists to answer these questions. For hundreds of years, Bushmen have understood the ways of animals like zebras and giraffes. They're very good wild animal trackers. The Bushmen know what the animals eat. They know where the animals go. They even know where they sleep.

However, there is a problem. The Bushmen don't always speak the same language as the conservationists. This can cause problems when they work together, and **communicating**[1] information is sometimes difficult. This is where new ideas and new technology can help.

---

[1]**communicate:** to share or exchange information by speaking or writing

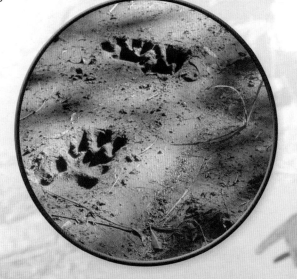

The Cyber Tracker is an invention created by Louis Liebenberg. Liebenberg has brought the invention to Karoo National Park in South Africa. He hopes that the Bushmen can help to protect the animals using the Cyber Tracker. He thinks it's a perfect match of modern technology and old knowledge. But what is the Cyber Tracker?

Liebenberg explains that it's a small computer that helps collect information about animals. It uses pictures, called 'icons', instead of words to record information. This way, the Bushmen can record what they see without words. They don't have to read or speak the same language as Liebenberg and other conservationists. According to Liebenberg, the Cyber Tracker can collect very detailed and **complicated**[1] information very quickly.

---

[1] **complicated:** difficult; with many parts

However, that's not the only thing the Cyber Tracker can do. The small computer also contains a **global positioning device**.[1] Each time a Bushman sees something interesting about an animal or plant, he pushes a button. The Cyber Tracker records exactly where the Bushman is. That way, even if the Bushman can't read or write, he can record what he sees and where. But how does the Cyber Tracker record information?

---

[1]**global positioning device (GPD):** a machine that tracks where things are on the earth

button

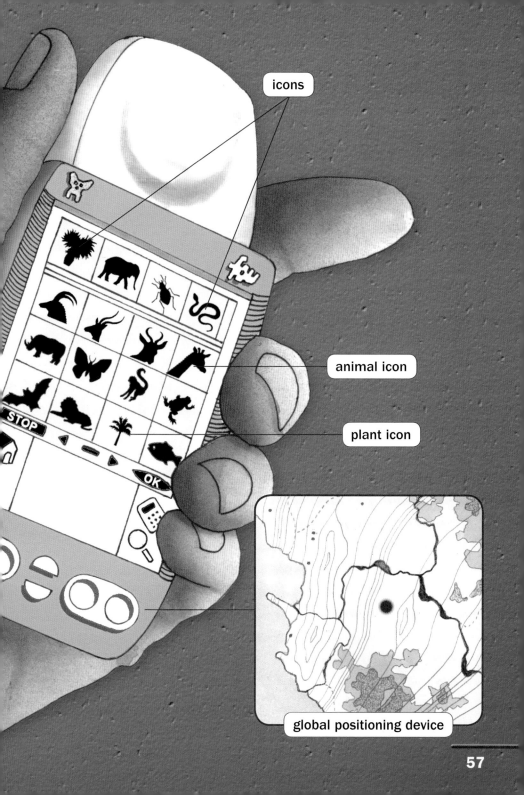

icons

animal icon

plant icon

STOP

OK

global positioning device

Liebenberg explains that the Cyber Tracker uses icons to communicate. There are pictures for drinking, walking, fighting, sleeping, eating, and other things. With the Cyber Tracker, the user can even report whether an animal is sick or dead. The Bushman can also record other meanings by pushing different buttons. With this **option**,[1] they can name about 50 different plants. This becomes very useful when the Bushmen want to record what the animals are eating.

However, Liebenberg adds that it's not just about the technology. According to him, the human **factor**[2] is also very important. Liebenberg says that a big part of using the Cyber Tracker is the Bushman's ability to record the information. He must be able to understand and correctly report everything he sees. The combination of machine and man seems to be working very well.

---

[1]**option:** a choice
[2]**factor:** sth that affects an event

When the trackers return to their **base**,[1] they connect the Cyber Tracker to a personal computer. Then, Liebenberg looks at the data and uses it to create maps. These maps show where the animal herds are. They also give information about what the animals are eating, and indicate facts about their health. Liebenberg can get a lot of detailed information about a lot of wild animals.

---

[1]**base:** the main place where one works, stays, or lives

The Cyber Tracker project started five years ago. At first, the idea was to help a few animals in danger. Because of this, the invention was used only in certain situations. Nowadays, the Cyber Tracker is used much more often. More and more people have started using the Cyber Tracker in other African parks. They have also started using it with many different kinds of animals.

Recently, Liebenberg has even put the Cyber Tracker **software**[1] on the Internet. Now many conservationists around the world can get the software. They have started adding the technology to their conservation programmes. The future of the Cyber Tracker looks good. Soon, it may be able to help in the conservation of wild animals everywhere.

---

[1]**software:** computer programme

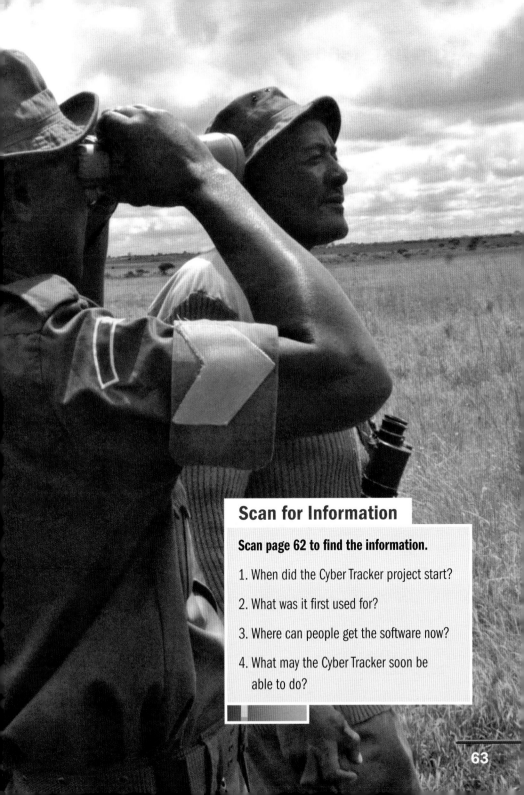

Scan for Information

Scan page 62 to find the information.

1. When did the Cyber Tracker project start?

2. What was it first used for?

3. Where can people get the software now?

4. What may the Cyber Tracker soon be able to do?

After You Read

1. Which of these is happening to herds of animals in Africa?
   A. Conservationists are moving them.
   B. They are in danger from the Cyber Tracker.
   C. They are increasing in number.
   D. The land they need is being taken.

2. On page 48, the phrase 'leading a fight' is closest in meaning to:
   A. working hard
   B. arguing
   C. disagreeing
   D. talking to people

3. Liebenberg thinks an important aim of conservation is:
   A. to know the exact number of animals in Africa.
   B. for people to understand more about plants and animals.
   C. to prove animal numbers in Africa are increasing.
   D. to count every plant.

4. The best heading for page 52 is:
   A. Conservationists Can't Answer Questions.
   B. Bushmen Know Too Much About Animals.
   C. Bushmen Use Software to Communicate.
   D. Bushmen Can Help Conservationists.

5. Bushmen know _____ about animals.
   A. very
   B. nothing
   C. a lot
   D. too

6. On page 52, who is 'they' in 'they sleep'?
   A. animals
   B. bushmen
   C. conservationists
   D. Liebenberg

7. The purpose of the Cyber Tracker is to:
   A. help with communication.
   B. record interesting facts.
   C. record complicated information.
   D. all of the above

8. How does the Cyber Tracker make communication easy?
   A. People can see where the Bushmen are.
   B. The invention uses pictures to communicate.
   C. The software can identify 50 different plants.
   D. Conservationists can track Bushmen.

9. The Cyber Tracker helps to make _____ about the animals and plants.
   A. trackers
   B. computers
   C. maps
   D. inventions

10. The original aim of the Cyber Tracker was to help a few animals.
   A. True
   B. False

11. The writer probably thinks that:
   A. technology is making conservation easier.
   B. the Cyber Tracker is difficult for conservationists.
   C. Louis Liebenberg is a famous software maker.
   D. every student should have the Cyber Tracker.

12. According to page 62, which of the following will <u>not</u> happen in the future?
   A. The Cyber Tracker will be added to other conservation programmes.
   B. The Cyber Tracker will be able to help animals everywhere.
   C. Conservationists won't be able to get the Cyber Tracker software.
   D. All of the above

DAILY News

GLOBAL POSITIONING DEVICES BECOME INCREASINGLY COMMON

The invention of the satellite over 50 years ago opened the way for the Global Positioning System (GPS). GPS uses a series of satellites to provide exact information about the location, or position, of certain objects. There are currently 24 GPS satellites in use. There are also three additional satellites if one of the 24 stops working. Originally, only the United States government was able to use the system. Today, however, people everywhere can use GPS technology for free. This is making Global Positioning Devices (GPDs) much more common.

GPS uses a series of satellites.

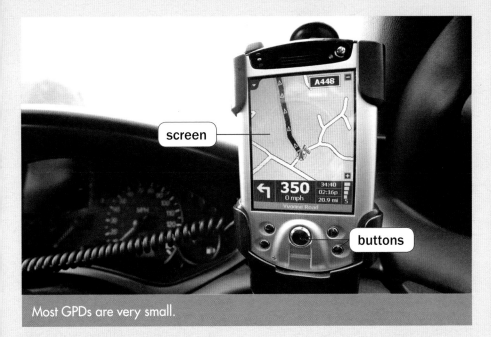

screen

buttons

Most GPDs are very small.

A GPD is usually a small machine with a screen and several buttons on the front. They are often about the size of a mobile phone. First, a GPD sends information to several satellites. This information tells the system where the user is; however, it must reach at least three satellites to work correctly. Next, GPS measures the GPD's exact distance from each satellite. It then sends this information back to the GPD. Finally, the GPD uses special software to change this information into a map with marks on it.

GPDs are like having a map that follows you wherever you go. They allow the user to see where he or she is at any moment. People can use the information to track where they have been or to plan where they want to go. Fishermen have discovered how useful GPDs can be when they are out on the open water. Many of today's new cars include GPDs. Drivers choose a destination and the GPD shows them the best way to get there. Some people are even placing GPDs on other people. They want to know where the person is at all times. The possible applications for GPDs are endless. Who knows where they'll turn up next?

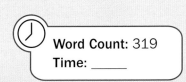

Word Count: 319
Time: _____

Grammar Focus: Expressing Obligation: *be expected to*; *be supposed to* (present tense)

- *am/is/are* + *supposed* + *to*-infinitive:
  To express a rule that needs to be followed:
  I am supposed to be at the party 10 minutes before the other guests.
- *am/is/are* + *expected* + *to*-infinitive:
  To express both obligation and what people hope or expect to happen:
  Christopher is expected to go to college after he graduates.
  To make a prediction about the future:
  The dollar is expected to get weaker.
- Use '*am/is/are supposed* + *to*-infinitive' in a way similar to *should*. This verb is not used in the active.
- Use '*am/is/are expected* + *to*-infinitive' to show what others hope will happen, to express obligation, or to talk about a predicted result.

Grammar Practice: Expressing Obligation: *be expected to*; *be supposed to* (present tense)

Match the columns to make the correct sentences.

1. Solar cookers are expected to ___

2. SCI is supposed to ___

3. Traditional fuels are expected to ___

4. Environmentalists are expected to ___

5. The cookers aren't supposed to ___

a. start having more workshops soon.

b. disappear.

c. change lives.

d. work for more than two years.

e. help SCI promote the cookers.

Grammar Focus: Expressing Purpose: *Use* with infinitives or *for* + gerund

- *Use* with infinitive: *You can <u>use</u> this knife (in order) <u>to cut</u> vegetables.*
- *Use* with *for* + gerund: *You can <u>use</u> this knife <u>for cutting</u> vegetables.*
- The infinitive of purpose expresses a purpose or a reason for something. It can be formed with or without the phrase *in order*.
- *For* + gerund also explains the purpose of an object.
- With the verb *use*, both forms are usually possible.

Grammar Practice: Expressing Purpose: *Use* with infinitives or *for* + gerund

Match the parts of the sentences to make true statements. On a separate piece of paper, rewrite the sentences replacing infinitives with *for* + gerund and *for* + gerund with infinitives.

1. In Spirit Lake, the wind is used for ___
2. The school can use the money they save ___
3. Silos are used on farms for ___
4. The school uses an electricity grid ___
5. Energy companies use farmers' land ___

a. storing food products.
b. making electricity.
c. to sell extra electricity.
d. to employ new teachers.
e. for building turbines.

Grammar Focus: Questions about Purpose: *Use* with *for* + gerund

What's a broom (used) for?   *It's (used) for cleaning floors.*

- Active questions: *What do you use a broom for?*
- Passive questions: *What is a broom (used) for?*
- The past participle *used* is often omitted in informal passive questions.

Grammar Practice: Questions about Purpose: *Use* with *for* + gerund
Match the questions with their answers.

1. What's a wind turbine used for?   ____

2. What are the steel rods used for?   ____

3. What's a blanket used for?   ____

4. What are scissors used for?   ____

5. What's this cream used for?   ____

a. They're used for cutting cloth and paper.

b. It's used for making your skin soft.

c. They're used for holding the turbine in place.

d. It's used for making electricity.

e. It's used for keeping you warm in bed.

Grammar Focus: Noun Clauses

	Noun clause		
	connector +	subject +	verb
	what	he	said.
	when	she	arrived.
I (don't) know	why	they	did that.
	where	he	went.
	how	she	got here.
	whether	they	understand.

- A noun clause takes the place of a noun phrase or pronoun in a sentence:
  I like the food. / I like <u>what you cooked</u>.
- A noun clause can have different grammatical functions in the sentence:
  Subject: <u>*What you cooked*</u> *tasted great.*
  Complement: *That was <u>what you cooked</u>.*
  Object: *I tasted <u>what you cooked</u>.*
  Object of preposition: *I thought about <u>what you cooked</u>.*

Grammar Practice: Noun Clauses

Complete the sentences with noun clauses. Use each connecting word only once.

what	when	why	how	where

e.g. Liebenberg invented the Cyber Tracker <u>five years ago</u>. I know
<u>*when Liebenberg invented the Cyber Tracker.*</u>

1. He moved to Africa <u>to help the animals</u>. I understand _____
   _____

2. Elephants communicate <u>with sounds</u>. I learned about _____
   _____

3. Lions eat <u>smaller animals</u>. I know _____
   _____

4. Giraffes live <u>in Africa</u>. I can tell you _____
   _____

Video Practice

A. A. Watch the video of *Solar Cooking* and write the word you hear.

1. 'A solar cooker needs only the light from the sun to cook meat, fish, grains, and vegetables – even if the _____ temperature isn't very hot.'
2. 'This method is becoming popular among people who are concerned about the environment. However, in developing _____, solar cookers can save lives.'
3. 'Their goals are to stop deforestation and to make women's lives _____.'
4. 'And the smoke from that fire, it burns their _____ and chokes their lungs.'

B. Watch the video again and circle the verb you hear.

1. 'With help from other human aid groups, Solar Cookers International has already trained more than 22,000 families how to (make/cook) traditional foods with the sun.'
2. 'After each workshop, attendees (are given/are allowed) their own portable solar "cook kits".'
3. 'SCI reports that solar cooking is also an effective way to make water pure and safe to (drink/use).'
4. 'Solar Cookers International has developed a useful measuring tool that helps people to (know/learn) when water is safe to drink.'
5. 'But SCI is not satisfied with just helping these people. Their goal is to (improve/increase) the use of solar cookers everywhere.'

Video Practice

C. Watch the video of *Wind Power* and circle the word you hear.

1. 'These turbines are helping the (schools/district) to save energy – and money.'
2. 'Since then, the school has (built/constructed) a second turbine.'
3. 'In extremely strong winds, the huge (hubs/blades) of the wind turbines simply shut down, or stop working.'
4. 'They'll produce (energy/electricity) in winds of just eight miles an hour.'
5. 'The larger turbine sends its power to the local (energy/ electricity) grid.'

D. Watch the video again and write down the word or number you hear.

1. 'In the countryside south of the Spirit Lake schools, more turbines stand near the big _____ on the local farms.'
2. 'Now, farmers can make _____ from the wind, just as they do from selling their crops.'
3. 'This piece of the Iowa countryside is just 27 miles long, but it now has _____ wind turbines.'
4. 'They write down the amounts of fossil fuels, such as _____, that are no longer needed for energy for the school.'
5. 'In this part of Iowa, people are using wind power to earn money and to learn about _____ the environment.'

Video Practice

E. Watch the video of *Wild Animal Trackers* and circle the word you hear.

1. 'But today many of these animals are in danger because people are taking the (land/space) that animals need.'
2. 'Conservationists are people who protect (animals/wildlife) and nature.'
3. 'The most important thing is to try and get an (understanding/idea) of what's happening out there.'
4. 'Each time a Bushman sees something (unusual/interesting) about an animal or plant, he pushes a button.'
5. 'Liebenberg adds that ... a big part of using the Cyber Tracker is the Bushman's ability to understand and record what he (sees/finds).'

F. Watch the video again and fill in the missing word

1. 'Liebenberg reports that people need to know more about _____.'
2. 'But, they don't always speak the same _____ as the conservationists ...'
3. 'That way, the Bushmen can record what they see even without _____.'
4. 'There are pictures for drinking, walking, fighting, sleeping, _____, and other things.'
5. 'At first, the idea was to help a few animals in _____.'

(1) The people at Solar Cookers International (SCI) have shown thousands of people how to cook food using the power of the sun. (2) A solar cooker is a cardboard box with shiny walls that direct the sunlight onto a pot inside the box. (3) The pot becomes warmer and warmer, and eventually it gets very hot. (4) Although cooking food is its main use, solar cookers can also be used to help people make water clean and safe to drink. (5) This is very important in many parts of the developing world. (6) In such countries, 6,000 people a day are dying of waterborne diseases. (7) These deaths could be prevented if people would pasteurise their drinking water. (8) By simply heating the water to 65° Celsius or 149° Fahrenheit, it becomes safe to drink. (9) Isn't it amazing that a five-dollar solar cooker can save so many lives?

A. Read the paragraph and answer the questions.

1. The purpose of this reading is to
   _____.
   A. describe waterborne illnesses
   B. encourage people to buy solar
   cookers for themselves
   C. show how solar cookers can
   provide safe drinking water
   D. explain the difference between
   Celsius and Fahrenheit

2. How many people are dying every
   day from drinking water that is not
   pure?
   A. 5,000
   B. 6,000
   C. 65,000
   D. 149,000

3. According to the reading, which of
   the following is most likely true?
   A. Heating water to 50° Celsius
   makes it safe to drink.
   B. The cardboard walls of a solar
   cooker sometimes get burnt.
   C. Solar cooking is very expensive.
   D. Solar cooking is slower than
   regular cooking.

4. The word 'it' in sentence 3 refers to
   _____.
   A. the cardboard box
   B. the pot
   C. the sunlight
   D. the developing world

5. The writer of the paragraph thinks that _____.
A. solar cookers are wonderful
B. solar cookers should work faster
C. solar cookers should be cheaper
D. solar cookers are ugly

6. Where should this sentence go?
In fact, it becomes hot enough to cook food.
A. after sentence 1
B. after sentence 3
C. after sentence 6
D. after sentence 8

B. Answer the questions.

7. A hard, black substance that is burned for energy is called _____.
A. cardboard
B. fuel
C. charcoal
D. cooker

8. A nation that is economically weak but growing is a _____ country.
A. developing
B. solar
C. workshop
D. waterborne

9. People _____ water to make sure it's safe to drink.
A. supposed boil
B. are supposed to boil
C. supposed to boiling
D. supposed boil

10. The football team _____ win the game.
A. expected
B. expecting to
C. is expected to
D. be expected to

(1) Wind turbines are huge energy-making machines that turn wind power into electrical power. **(2)** The larger turbine in a town called Spirit Lake in the U.S. state of Iowa is 180 feet tall. **(3)** It has steel legs that go 25 feet down into the ground. **(4)** It needs this solid support because the wind in this area is sometimes very strong. **(5)** It has been measured at up to 130 miles per hour. **(6)** There are even tornados in Iowa from time to time and this turbine must be able to survive them. **(7)** I wouldn't want to be around during one of those! **(8)** Surprisingly, the larger turbine is also able to handle very light winds. **(9)** The smaller turbine at Spirit Lake supplies energy directly to the area's schools while the large one sends its power to an electricity grid. **(10)** This extra power is stored there so that it can be used or sold later on.

A. Read the paragraph and answer the questions.

11. Which of the following is probably true?
   A. Spirit Lake sometimes uses power from the electricity grid.
   B. There are more than two wind turbines in Spirit Lake.
   C. The wind turbine can make electricity with a five-mile-per-hour wind.
   D. The larger turbine sometimes supplies electricity to the area's schools.

12. How big is the larger turbine?
   A. 8 feet tall
   B. 25 feet tall
   C. 130 feet tall
   D. 180 feet tall

13. According to the paragraph, the writer _____.
   A. wants Spirit Lake to build more turbines.
   B. is afraid of tornados
   C. thinks that the larger turbine is too tall
   D. once experienced a tornado

14. Where should this sentence go? It can produce electricity when the wind is blowing at only eight miles per hour.
   A. after sentence 2
   B. after sentence 5
   C. after sentence 8
   D. after sentence 10

15. The word 'it' in sentence 5 refers
to _____.

B. Answer the questions.

16. People often use mobile phones
_____ to people they are
meeting at the airport.
A. talking
B. talk
C. to talk
D. talked

17. An extremely strong wind that
blows in a circle is called a

_____.
A. wind turbine
B. tornado
C. countryside
D. fossil fuel

18. Decide which underlined word
is incorrect.
I <u>use</u> my rucksack <u>for</u> carry
everything I <u>need</u> for <u>doing</u> my
homework.
A. use
B. for
C. need
D. doing

C. Read the sentences. Write 'True' or 'False'. Refer to the paragraph if
necessary.

19. The legs of the turbine must go deep into the ground because the
turbines are very efficient. _____
20. A blade is a thin, wide part of a machine used to push air or water.
_____

(1) The Cyber Tracker is a special type of computer that helps conservationists collect important information about animals. (2) Conservationists in Africa are teaching some Bushmen how to use it. (3) The Bushmen don't speak the same language as the scientists so the computer uses pictures, not words. (4) For example, there are pictures on it for drinking, walking, sleeping, and eating. (5) There are also other sets of pictures showing a variety of animals and plants. (6) The Bushmen record information by pushing the picture buttons. (7) This gives the conservationists a lot of information about what the animals are doing and what they are eating. (8) The Cyber Tracker does something else that's very useful. (9) It contains a global positioning device that tells the scientists exactly where the Bushman was when he recorded the information. (10) Even though a Bushman might not be able to read or write, he can record and communicate a great deal of useful information. (11) Conservationists use this information to make maps showing where, and how, the animals live. (12) These maps help the conservationists to do their important job.

A. Read the paragraph and answer the questions.

21. The Cyber Tracker shows where the Bushman was because _____.

    A. it uses pictures, not words
    B. it contains a global positioning device
    C. it is very small
    D. it has pictures of animals and plants

22. What is the main idea of this paragraph?

    A. how the Cyber Tracker system works
    B. why the Cyber Tracker system uses pictures
    C. which animals are helped by the Cyber Tracker
    D. why the Bushmen haven't learned to read and write

23. According to the paragraph, the writer believes that _____.
  A. Cyber Trackers should not use pictures
  B. the scientists should do more to help the Bushmen
  C. Cyber Trackers are not very useful
  D. protecting animals is important work

24. Where should this sentence go? In fact, there are pictures of about 50 different kinds of plants in the Cyber Tracker.
  A. after sentence 2
  B. after sentence 5
  C. after sentence 9
  D. after sentence 11

25. The word 'it' in sentence 9 refers to _____.
  A. the Cyber Tracker
  B. the global positioning device
  C. a plant
  D. some information

26. The paragraph says there are pictures of _____ on the Cyber Tracker.
  A. rivers
  B. hills
  C. Bushmen
  D. plants

B. Answer the questions.

27. A group of animals is called a _____.
  A. herd
  B. track
  C. language
  D. map

28. The elephant is a _____ animal.
  A. fast-moving
  B. black and white
  C. small, red
  D. large, grey

29. Which sentence is grammatically correct?
  Do they know …
  A. where the herds are?
  B. when will the giraffes returning?
  C. how much eat the elephants?
  D. why has the giraffe such long legs?

30. Which sentence is grammatically correct?
  A. I asked what language speak the Bushmen.
  B. He asked how the Bushmen did learn so much about animals.
  C. They asked why the Bushmen were using Cyber Trackers.
  D. He asked how works the Cyber Tracker.

Key 答案

Solar Cooking
Words to Know: A. 1. solar **2.** cooker **3.** cardboard **4.** Workshops
B. 1. microbiologist **2.** deforestation **3.** Charcoal **4.** Waterborne
5. developing country **6.** Fuels **7.** pasteurise
Predict: open answers
Summarise: open answers
After You Read:1. B **2.** C **3.** A **4.** C **5.** A **6.** D **7.** A **8.** D **9.** C **10.** B **11.** A
12. A

Wind Power
Words to Know: A. 1. f **2.** c **3.** a **4.** d **5.** b **6.** e **B. 1.** silo **2.** countryside
3. crops **4.** tornado
Predict: 1. False **2.** True **3.** True
Summarise: open answers
After You Read: 1. B **2.** C **3.** D **4.** A **5.** C **6.** A **7.** B **8.** A **9.** B **10.** C **11.** B
12. B

Wild Animal Trackers
Words to Know: A. 1. herd **2.** giraffes **3.** zebras **4.** animal tracks
5. elephants **B.** (suggested answers) **1.** a system of written or verbal
communication **2.** someone who protects animals or plants
3. equipment or machines based on modern science.
Summarise: (suggested answers) **1.** Having information about animals
will help with their protection. **2.** People should know how plants and
animals change over time.
Scan for Information: 1. five years ago **2.** to help a few animals in danger
3. on the Internet **4.** help in the conservation of wild animals everywhere
After You Read: 1. D **2.** A **3.** B **4.** D **5.** C **6.** A **7.** D **8.** B **9.** C **10.** A **11.** A
12. C

Grammar Practice

Expressing Obligation: 1. c **2.** a **3.** b **4.** e **5.** d
Expressing Purpose: 1. b **2.** d **3.** a **4.** c **5.** e
Questions about Purpose: 1. d **2.** c **3.** e **4.** a **5.** b
Noun Clauses: 1. why he moved to Africa **2.** how elephants communicate
3. what lions eat **4.** where giraffes live

Video Practice

A. 1. air **2.** countries **3.** easier **4.** eyes **B. 1.** cook **2.** are given **3.** drink
4. know **5.** increase **C. 1.** schools **2.** constructed **3.** blades **4.** energy
5. electricity **D. 1.** silos **2.** money **3.** 257 **4.** coal **5.** saving **E. 1.** land
2. wildlife **3.** understanding **4.** interesting **5.** sees **F. 1.** animals
2. language **3.** words **4.** eating **5.** danger

Exit Test

1. C **2.** B **3.** D **4.** B **5.** A **6.** B **7.** C **8.** A **9.** B **10.** C **11.** A **12.** D **13.** B
14. C **15.** wind, the wind **16.** C **17.** B **18.** B **19.** False **20.** True **21.** B
22. A **23.** D **24.** B **25.** A **26.** D **27.** A **28.** D **29.** A **30.** C

English - Chinese Vocabulary List 中英對照生詞表
(Arranged in alphabetical order)

absorb	吸收	kit	工具套
alternative	供替代的選擇	model	模型
base	基地	option	選擇
brilliant	卓越的	pay off	全部償清
carbon dioxide	二氧化碳	pasteurisation	加熱殺菌法
choke (one's) lungs	使(某人)窒息	physics	物理學
communicate	溝通	portable	手提式的
complicated	複雜	remarkable	非凡的
conservationist	天然資源保護論者	school district	學校區
consistency	軟硬度	significant	重要的
construct	興建	software	軟件
consume	食用	stand up to	抵禦
deforestation	砍伐樹木	stove	爐子
efficient	有效率的	sulphur dioxide	二氧化硫
equipment	設備	superintendent	校長
experiment	試驗	technology	科技
factor	因素	texture	口感 / 質地
founding member	創辦人	tornado	龍捲風
global positioning device (GPD)	全球定位裝置	valuable	值錢的
impressive	非常多	wax	蠟
indicate	顯示	wild	野生的
issue	爭議	withstand	抵擋
kicking pretty good	吹得快	World Health Organization (WHO)	世界衛生組織